Kit Visits the Farm

Story by Lori Mortensen

Illustrations by Nikki Boetger

One spring day, Kit invited her friend Leo to go with her on a trip.

"Where are you going?" asked Leo.

"To Uncle Ray's farm," said Kit.
"It's the best place ever!"

3

At the farm, Kit couldn't wait to show Leo all the fun things to do.

On the first day, they climbed trees, skipped rocks, and swam in the pond.

On the second day, they played on the tire swing, went fishing, and jumped in the hay.

"I could stay here forever!" said Leo.

"Me too!" said Kit.

The next morning, Kit and Leo ran out of ideas for things to do.

"What should we do today?" asked Leo.

Kit shrugged.

While fixing breakfast, Uncle Ray
told them about a new lamb.
He had found it early that morning.
It had been born the night before.

"We have so many new baby animals on the farm," said Uncle Ray. "I need to count them all."

Kit and Leo looked at each other.

"We could count them!" said Kit.

"We could keep track of them in my notebook," said Leo.

Kit and Leo ran to the red barn.

They counted
two white lambs,

one black colt,

and three brown calves.

"They're really big babies!" said Kit.

After lunch, Kit and Leo counted six pink piglets,

eight spotted puppies,

and nine baby gray rabbits.

"Wow!" exclaimed Leo.
"There are a lot of baby rabbits."

"Look at their wiggly noses!" said Kit.

Near the pond, Kit and Leo counted four little green frogs and ten striped ducklings.

"It looks like a parade!" said Kit.

Next, Kit and Leo counted five black-and-white baby goats

and seven yellow chicks.

When Kit and Leo finished, they looked at their notebook pages.

"Now let's put the numbers in order," said Kit.

"One black colt,
two white lambs,
three brown calves,
four little green frogs,
and five black-and-white
baby goats," said Leo.

Kit continued, "Six pink piglets,
seven yellow chicks,
eight spotted puppies,
nine baby gray rabbits ..."

7 Chicks

8 Puppies

9 Rabbits

10 Ducklings

NOTEBOOK

Just then, the duck family waddled by.

"Here comes the parade!" said Leo.

Kit counted, "One, two, three, four, five, six, seven, eight, nine—"

"Wait," said Kit. "Weren't there ten ducklings?"

"You're right," said Leo.
"One of the ducklings is missing!"

"We have to find it," said Kit.

Kit and Leo searched around the pond,
but the duckling wasn't there.

Next, they searched in the barn,

in the goat pen,

and the pigsty.

"It's not here,"
said Leo.

Then Kit and Leo looked in the rabbit hutch and the chicken coop, but they could not find the duckling.

"Where could it be?" said Kit.

Then Kit and Leo heard a bark.

"Come on," said Kit. "There's one place we forgot to look!"

Kit and Leo raced to the doghouse.

Kit laughed.
"There used to be eight puppies, but now there are nine!"

Kit and Leo returned the duckling to its mother.

"Ten ducklings!" said Kit, proudly.

Later, Kit and Leo showed Uncle Ray their notebook pages.

"You counted a lot of babies!" said Uncle Ray. "Thank you!"

"It was fun," said Kit.

"You were right about the farm, Kit," said Leo. "It *is* the best place ever!"

Glossary

rabbit

frog

lamb

calf

puppy

piglet

colt

duckling

goat

chick

barn

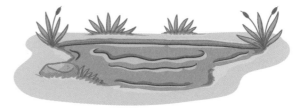

pond

The Learnalots™

Bo
Literacy

Kit
Math

Piper
Music and Movement

Sofie
Social and Emotional Skills

Flora
Nature

Scout
Health and Fitness

Leo
Science

Zak
Art and Creativity

BrightStart Learning
7342 11th Ave. NW
Seattle, WA 98117
www.brightstartlearning.com

Developed in conjunction with Trillium Publishing, Inc.

Illustrations created by Nikki Boetger.

ISBN: 978-1-938751-07-3

Printed and bound in China.

10 9 8 7 6 5 4 3 2 1